For Sadie and the nurses of Ward 3

Library of Congress Cataloging in Publication Data

Stone, Bernard.
  Emergency mouse.
  SUMMARY: A young boy who is hospitalized discovers
that a group of mice operate a hospital of their own in
the wall of his room.
  [1. Hospitals—Fiction. 2. Mice—Fiction]
I. Steadman, Ralph. II. Title.
PZ7.S87594Em   [E]   78-7397
ISBN 0-13-274555-0

*Emergency Mouse Story by Bernard Stone Illustrations by Ralph Steadman Copyright © 1978 by Anderson Press
Ltd. First American edition published 1978 by Prentice-Hall, Inc. All rights reserved. No part of this book may be
reproduced in any form or by any means, except for the inclusion of brief quotations in a review, without permission
in writing from the publisher. Printed in Italy by Grafiche AZ, Verona J Prentice-Hall International, Inc.,
London Prentice-Hall of Australia, Pty. Ltd., North Sydney Prentice-Hall of Canada, Ltd., Toronto Prentice-Hall
of India Private Ltd., New Delhi Prentice-Hall of Japan, Inc., Tokyo Prentice-Hall of Southeast Asia Pte. Ltd.,
Singapore 10 9 8 7 6 5 4 3 2 1*

EMERGENCY MOUSE

by Bernard Stone
Illustrated by Ralph Steadman

Prentice-Hall, Inc.
Englewood Cliffs, New Jersey

It was midnight. The ward was dark and quiet. All the patients were sound asleep—except for Henry.
He was in the hospital for an operation. His bed was very comfortable and warm, but the pain in his jaw was keeping him awake.
He tried to think of all the things he liked doing best.
Then he remembered his pet mouse, Whitey. On the day Henry had come to the hospital, the mouse had been very sick. Henry hoped that his mother was keeping a watchful eye over him.

Henry missed his mother. But he didn't want to think about it so he turned over on his side and tried to go to sleep. Just as he was closing his eyes, he noticed the strangest thing. There was a long row of tiny lights above little doors in the baseboard.

Then suddenly the doors opened and mice dressed as doctors and nurses came marching out, wheeling a row of little beds full of little mice patients. Henry couldn't believe his eyes—he leaned over the edge of his bed to get a closer look.

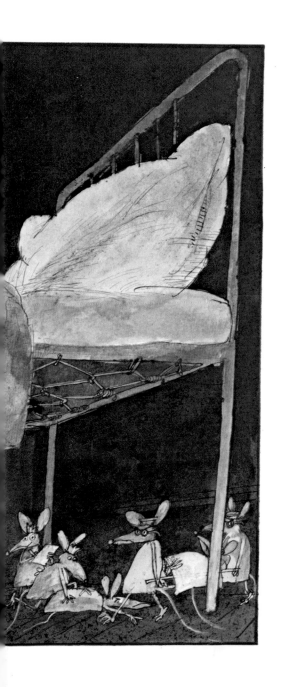

The mice were setting up their own hospital for the night. It was just like a human's hospital, except everything was in miniature and everywhere were mice. It was a mouse ward with a mouse surgeon and doctors and mouse nurses to take care of all the mouse patients.

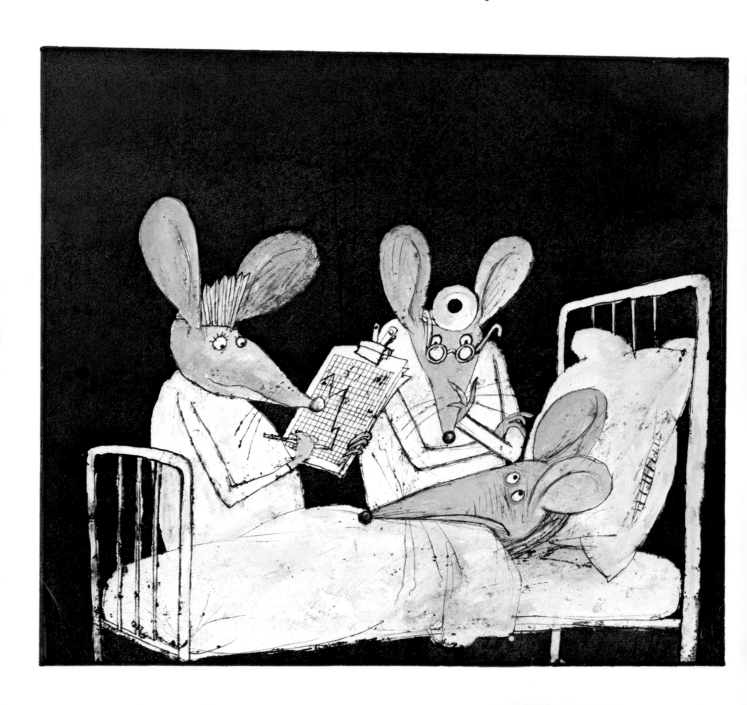

There was Fatty Mouse, who naturally was overweight. He was put on a liquid diet and the doctor said he would soon be much thinner.

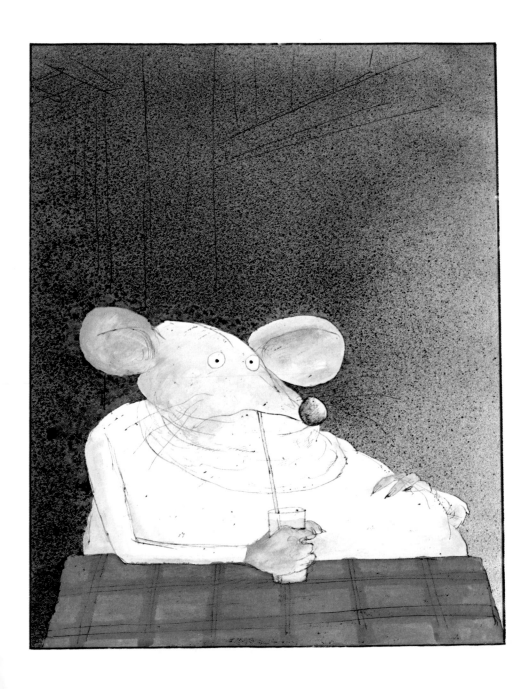

In the next bed was Toothy Mouse. He had raided a candy store and was now waiting to see the dentist.

Poor Limping Mouse hadn't been quite quick enough and a cat had caught him by the leg. But he was making good progress learning to walk with crutches.

Tropical Mouse had stowed away on a ship from foreign ports.
He was suffering from a rare tropical disease. He was the
yellowest mouse you ever saw.

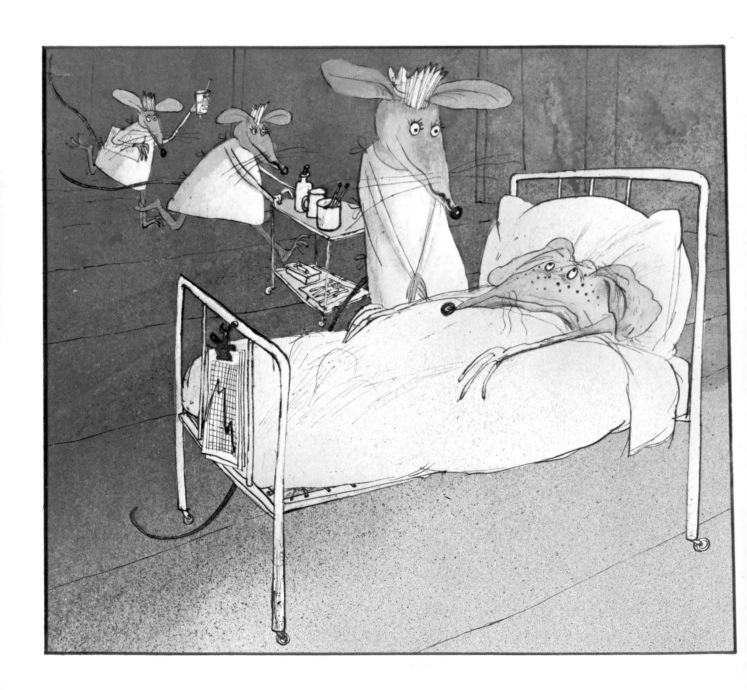

Hypochondriac Mouse was back again. He was always in and out of the hospital. He thought he had every illness in the medical dictionary. The doctors let him stay a few days each time and then sent him home.

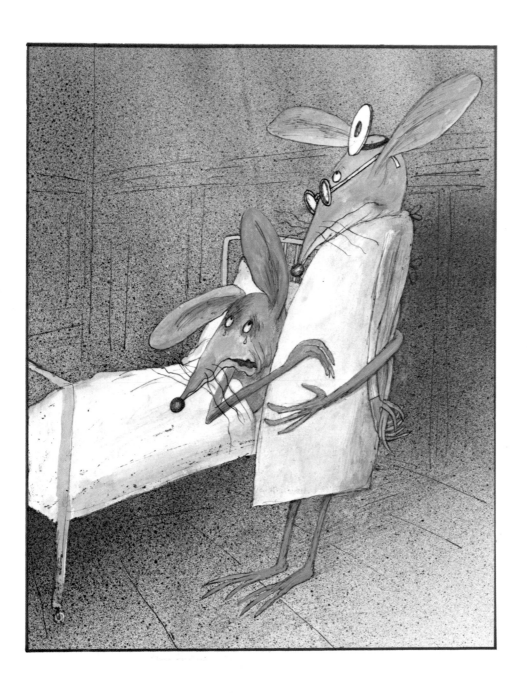

"Emergency here! Get him to the operating room at once!" It was Surgeon Mouse speaking. Champion Mouse, the daredevil cheese-stealer, had been caught in the act at last and he was brought in with a mousetrap firmly gripping his tail.

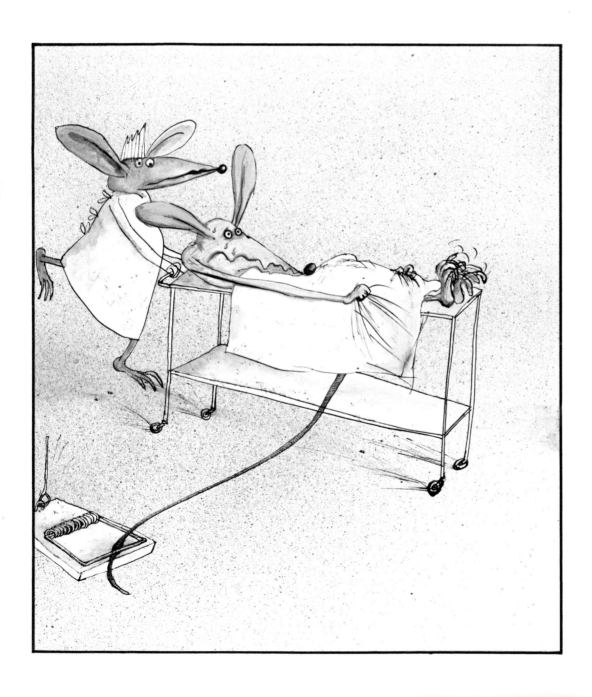

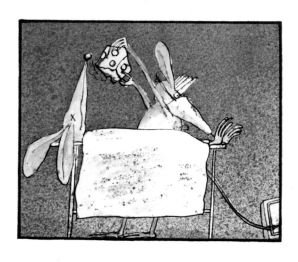

"Anaesthetic," Surgeon Mouse demanded, and Nurse Mouse held a large piece of cheese under Champion Mouse's nose. He fell asleep at once.

His tail was soon set free from the trap and put into splints.

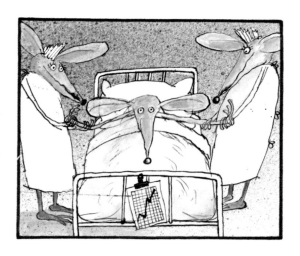

When he awoke he was back in his own bed, in the ward, and two Mouse Nurses were holding his hands.

Champion Mouse recovered very quickly. He was impatient to go hunting along that cheese trail again.

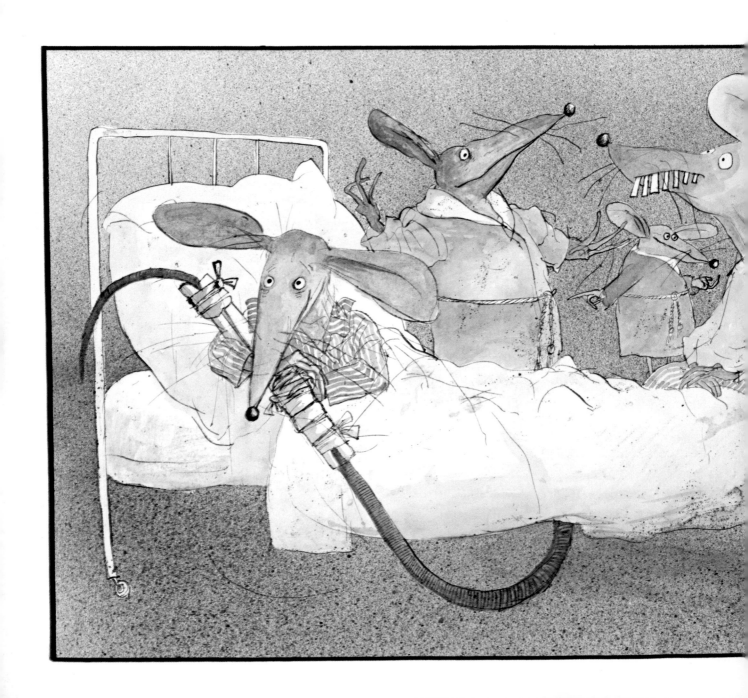

As the patients gathered around his bed, Champion Mouse thought he heard something. "Shsh!" he said. "I hear the sound of squeaky footsteps on the polished floor. It must be morning. Hurry, get all the beds back inside. I will make sure we have left everything the way it was."

Putting on his bright red tartan bathrobe,
Champion Mouse raced along the ward, but he
nearly collided with a huge noisy monster
coming towards him.

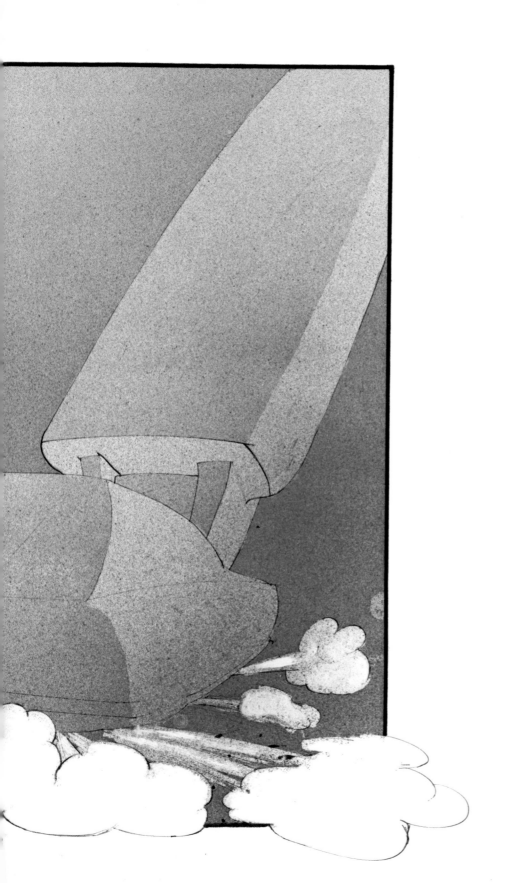

He darted out of the way—
only to bump into a broom that
was leaning against the wall.

The machine roared by again. He
climbed up the broom handle but
when he reached the windowsill,
a gust of air nearly blew him off.
Someone had switched on an
electric fan.

Then a radio was turned on. By this time he really had a headache. But he had to escape before it was too late.

He slid down the broom handle, under a serving cart and around an oxygen tank.

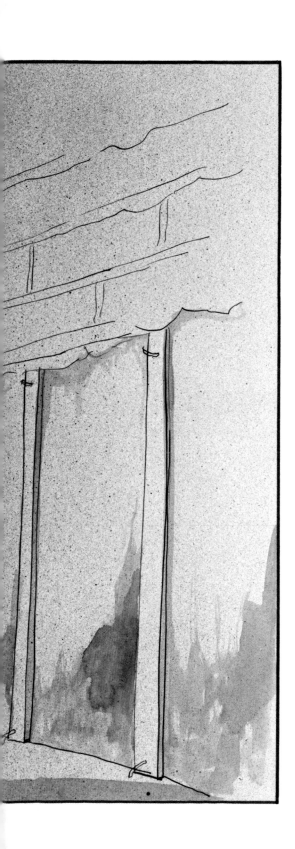

Breathlessly, he reached safety
and darted behind the baseboard
just as the lights went on.

Henry awoke. The early dawn sunlight was shining through the avenue of trees outside the bay windows in front of him. He stretched, yawned, and sat up as a nurse came towards him pushing the early morning teacart.

"Good morning, Henry. Did you sleep well?" she asked.
Henry glanced at the baseboard, smiled, and answered, "Yes, thank you, nurse, I slept very well, very well indeed."

"That's good," she smiled, "because the doctor said you were better. Your mother phoned and sent her love. She will be coming to take you home today."

"And," she continued, "I promised her that I would tell you right away that your white mouse is well again, too."